Sticky Fingers

by Meredith Costain

illustrated by David Dickson

The Characters

This is me.
Tony Angrilli,
part-time detective!

Dad
I work for him.

The motorbike guy

Nathan
He is the leader of
the Hornet gang.

The Setting

CONTENTS

Chapter 1
It all started out
like any other
Saturday morning 2

Chapter 2
Some people are
sooo rude! 12

Chapter 3
There are some people you
just don't tangle with . . 24

Chapter 4
Maybe the thief
has left a clue 38

Chapter 5
Tony Angrilli,
detective! 52

CHAPTER

It all started out like any other Saturday morning ...

What do you do on Saturday mornings? Sleep in? Watch cartoons on TV? Not me.

I have to work in my parents'
newsagency. I stack the papers and
magazines. I help customers find
what they want. It's okay because
I get paid for it.

At ten to nine I flicked off the TV and grabbed my bike. I rode down the lane, through the tunnel, and over the hill.

As I rode, I kept a lookout for any signs of crime. That's my hobby, you see. I want to be a detective when I leave school.

Dad reckons we live in a good area for it. Crime, that is. There have been a lot of house and car break-ins lately.

As I turned into Pine Street a
football went flying past my head.
Only one person I know can kick a
football that hard — Vinnie Pappas.

"Whoops!" called Vinnie. The ball soared over a brick wall and landed in someone's front garden.

"I'll get it!" I called to Vinnie. I felt like a bit of a kick.

I peered over the wall. A guy was
on the front lawn, working on his
motorbike. He was wearing an old
leather jacket with a sheepskin lining.
A jacket like that would be perfect
for when I get my trail bike.

The guy came to the wall. "Is this your ball?" he asked.

"Er ... it's my friend's," I said. "He's got a big kick."

"You're not kidding," he said as he handed me the ball. "Excuse my hands. They're a bit greasy from the bike."

"Okay," I said, kicking the ball to Vinnie.

"Meet you at the shop later, Vinnie," I called. "I've got to go now. I'm late for work."

Some people are *sooo* rude!

Dad scowled at me as I came in through the door. There were a lot of people waiting to be served.

"You're late again, Tony," Dad said.
"One more time and I'll find someone
else to do your job!"

"Sorry, Dad," I said.

Whoops. That was close. No job means
no money. And no money means no
trail bike. I quickly tidied up the
postcard stand.

An old lady began to look through the cards. "I'm trying to find a card for my niece," she said. "I can't seem to find the right one."

I pointed to some cards that had pictures of flowers and sunsets on them. My sister likes that sort of stuff.

"No, that's not what I want," she said grumpily.

Some people are *sooo* rude!

"Tony!" called my dad. "Can you get some more newspapers? They're nearly all gone."

I grabbed a stack of papers from the back room. I cut through the thick tape with Dad's knife, then took them to the rack.

"You there," demanded a rude voice. It was the old lady again. She'd made a mess of the newspapers. "Find me a paper that doesn't leave ink on my hands!"

There was nothing I could do. All the papers were the same.

Hey! There was the guy from this morning, the motorbike guy. He was leafing through a *Two Wheels* magazine.

"Hi!" I said. "Remember me?"

He didn't. He turned his back on me and kept reading.

What was wrong with everyone today?

The motorbike guy was still wearing his jacket. Up close, it didn't look so good. The leather was ripped and the lining was old. There were bits of sheepskin coming off.

His hands were still really greasy too. Yuk! He'd better not get grease all over the magazines. Dad would hit the roof!

There are some people you just
don't tangle with ...

Five kids trooped into the shop.
It was the Hornets. Just my bad luck.

The Hornets are this gang of kids
at school. They think they're really
tough. They hang around the shopping
centre giving shopkeepers a hard
time.

Last week it was the café. This week
it was us.

Nathan flicked me on the back of the head with his fingers.

"Hey, guys, it's Toe-nail," he smirked. "Working in Daddy's shop. Good boy, Toe-nail."

My fingers curled into fists, but
there was no point doing anything,
no point at all. I watched as Nathan
picked up a pile of cards and let
them slide to the floor.

Two of the Hornet girls went up to the lolly counter.

"I'll have two Mars Bars and a Cherry Ripe," said Josie.

"I'll have three Mars Bars, a Violet Crumble and a Crunchie," said Danka at the same time.

"No wait, I'll have four Crunchies and a packet of M&Ms," said Danka.

Poor old Dad looked really annoyed. "I wish you girls would make up your minds," he said.

"Oh, all right," sighed Josie. "Give me ... one Mars Bar."

Josie handed Dad some coins.

Suddenly there was a loud crash from the back of the shop. One of the Hornet boys had knocked over a whole shelf of magazines.

Dad ran down to the back of the shop.

"You boys! Get out of my shop. Now!" he screamed.

The Hornet boys skidded round the
magazines and took off out the door.

I stayed out of the way. If you'd ever tangled with the Hornets, you'd know why! I like having all my teeth and arms and legs in the right places.

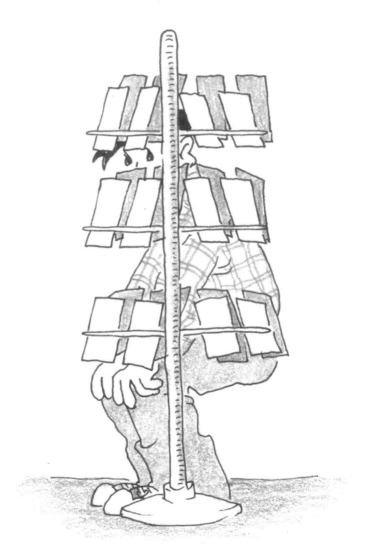

The Hornet girls gave Dad a big smile,
then walked slowly out of the shop.
The old lady walked out too.

Dad came back looking angry.

"Looks like someone dropped something," said Dad as he leant over to pick it up. He waved it at me. "Ten pounds!"

He walked around to the back of the counter.

"Tony!" he yelled. "Those rotten kids! They've stolen all the money from the till!"

Maybe the thief has left a clue ...

I raced over to the counter. The till was open. Open — and empty.

"Now I get it," said Dad. "The boys made a big noise at the back of the shop to get me away from the till. Then the girls took the money."

The Hornet gang? Robbing the till?
They'd never gone that far before.

"Did you see the girls take the money?"
I asked Dad.

"No, I didn't see them," said Dad.
He was really angry.

"Who else could it have been? If you'd been on time this morning, maybe this would never have happened!"

Huh? Now he was trying to blame me.

"Hi, Tony," said a voice behind me.

I spun round. Vinnie! He sure knew the wrong time to visit.

"Someone's taken the money out of the till," I told him.

"Yeah?" Vinnie said. "Who?"

"We're not sure," I told him, "but I'm going to find out."

Here was a chance to put my detective skills into action. Maybe the thief had left a clue!

I turned to Dad, "Can I have a look at that ten pound note?"

Dad handed me the note. I looked at it closely. There were a couple of black patches on it.

"What do you think these are?"
I asked Vinnie.

"Dirt?" Vinnie suggested.

"Or printer's ink, maybe?" I said.
I was thinking of the rude old lady
with the ink on her hands. She could
have left inky marks on the notes
when she grabbed them out of the
till!

I held the note up and took a deep
sniff. I knew that smell! It was ...
ummm ...

"Dad, what does this smell like?"
I said, waving the ten pound note
under his nose.

"Grease," he suggested.

Grease! Yes, of course, but I needed more proof. I knelt down and checked the floor behind the counter. Aha!

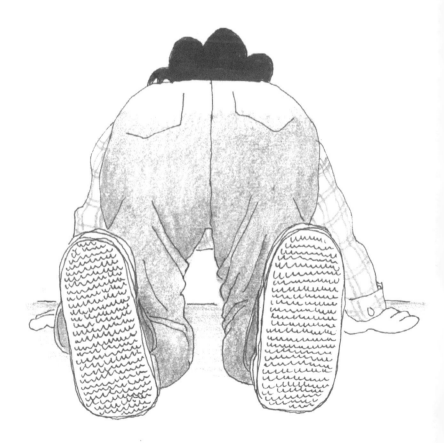

I waved a piece of sheepskin at Dad.
"Got him!" I said. "I know who the
thief is now!"

CHAPTER 5

Tony Angrilli, detective!

Dad looked surprised.
"You know who the thief is?" he asked.

"Sure," I said. "I even know where he lives! It's the motorbike guy. I met him this morning. His hands were all greasy from working on his bike. His fingerprints are all over this note."

"We'd better show it to the police," said Dad. "What's that bit of sheepskin got to do with it?"

"It's from his jacket," I explained. "I noticed parts of the lining falling out when he was looking at the magazines."

Dad gave me a big hug.
"Tony," he grinned, "you're a genius.
You deserve a reward for this."

"Thanks, Dad," I said. I grinned at
Vinnie. A reward, hey?

Maybe I was going to get that trail bike sooner than I'd thought!

GLOSSARY

clue
a hint

crime
breaking the law

customer
someone who buys things

detective
someone who
solves crimes

grumpily
in a cross way

hobby
something you like to do
in your own time

ink
used by printers
and for writing

sheepskin
the woolly skin
from a sheep

skid
to slide

till
where the money
is kept in a shop

Meredith Costain

What is your favourite breakfast?

Eggs, bacon and mushrooms on pancakes with lashings of maple syrup.

Who is your favourite cartoon character?

Daffy Duck. He's so 'de-shpicable'.

What was your least favourite activity at school?

Long division.

Why is the sky blue?

So red aeroplanes don't get lost.

David Dickson

What is your favourite breakfast?

Porridge with golden syrup.

Who is your favourite cartoon character?

Daffy Duck.

What was your least favourite activity at school?

Playground duty.

Why is the sky blue?

Because blue is a perfect colour.